Mary Chapman is an established children's and young adult author who has also written picture books for young children. After attending University College London and Leeds University, she taught English in secondary schools. After some years in teaching, Mary decided to train as a social worker and, later, as a family therapist.

In recent years Mary has achieved her ambition to become a writer. When she is not writing she enjoys discussing books with friends in a book group, art exhibitions, aerobics, walking, and gardening, although she would rather look at other people's gardens than work in her own.

Cold Fusion is a new series for readers who are curious, who enjoy a challenge and who like thinking outside the box.

Paupers

Mary Chapman

Paupers
by Mary Chapman

Published by Ransom Publishing Ltd.
Radley House, 8 St. Cross Road, Winchester, Hampshire SO23 9HX, UK
www.ransom.co.uk

ISBN 978 178127 576 4
First published in 2013

A CIP catalogue record of this book is available from the British Library.

Contents

One

The iron door-knocker, shaped like a fist, glinted in the moonlight. Beneath it huddled three figures, shivering in the cold wind that swept across the fields. Behind them, muddy lanes and bare hedgerows. Before them, high walls, a locked and bolted door.

'I'll knock, Mam,' said the boy.

He reached up, grasped the cold metal and banged it against the door.

They waited. Silence. The other two figures moved closer together. One of them held a bundle in her arms. The boy tried again, pounding the knocker against the door with all his strength.

A rattling of chains, and a sliding of bolts. The door creaked open. A sliver of light shone out.

'Who's there?' said a rough, male voice.

'Lydia Maddison and children, sir, from Cranby, sir.'

'Who sent you?'

'Relieving Officer, sir.'

'Where's your husband? Or ain't you got one? Are these all your bastards?'

The woman flinched.

'Our father's gone and left us,' the boy said. 'We've nowhere to go.'

'How many of you?'

'Three – me and my daughter and my son – and a babby,' the woman said.

'You can come in tonight, but you'll have to go in front of the Board tomorrow.'

The door opened wider and they stumbled in.

A thick-set, grim-faced man stood in front of them.

'You, boy, come with me. And you two can wait here. Mrs Scrimshaw, Assistant Matron, will deal with you.'

'But we're together,' Lydia said. 'We're a family.'

'Not here you're not. You're paupers. We don't let families live together in here no more. And quite right too.'

'But we've as much right to be together as a family as rich folk,' Lydia said. 'Just because we've fallen on hard times ... '

'It's the new Poor Law. It stops idle folk coming in here to live off the Parish in the lap of luxury while decent, hard-working souls struggle to earn a crust.'

'Mam,' the girl whispered, 'I don't want to stay here if we can't be together.'

'No, Mam, nor do I,' said the boy.

'Then be on your way.' The man threw open the door. 'There's plenty of others who'll be grateful for a bed.'

Lydia looked out into the dark night. Bare branches of trees tossed and swayed in the wind. Clouds covered the moon. She shook her head.

'We've nowhere else to go,' she said. 'We've no choice. We'll stay.'

The man slammed the door shut.

'Very well. Now, boy, you come along with me.'

'Where are you taking him?' Lydia tried to step between the boy and the man, but the man pushed her aside.

'To get out of them mucky clothes and into some clean 'uns,' he said. 'My missus'll do the same with you. Come on, boy. What's yer name?'

'Tom.'

'Tom what?'

'Tom Maddison.'

'Tom Maddison what?' the man shouted.

'Say *sir*,' Lydia whispered.

'Tom Maddison, sir.'

'It'll be Maddison here, and I'm M*r* Scrimshaw to you.'

He pushed Tom in front of him. The boy turned to look back over his shoulder at his mother.

'Go along with Mr Scrimshaw, Tom, there's a good lad.' Lydia tried to smile.

Scrimshaw gave Tom another shove, harder this time, so the boy stumbled. Lydia saw the smirk on Scrimshaw's face before he turned away to march after Tom down the dimly-lit passage.

In the opposite direction, at the far end of the passage, in the flickering gaslight, Lydia could see a dark shape approaching. It was a woman in a long, black dress and apron, with a bunch of keys at her waist – Mrs Scrimshaw.

'Follow me,' she said, as she reached Lydia and her daughter, 'and hurry up about it.'

'Come on, Rose.' Lydia put an arm round her daughter.

Rose clasped her bundle tightly, and they followed Mrs Scrimshaw along the passage.

At last she stopped by a door, selected a key from the bunch that rattled at her waist, unlocked the door and pushed it open.

'In here. Hurry! Hurry!' she snapped.

Lydia had hoped to see beds, or at least a mattress on the floor. She was desperately tired and she knew Rose was exhausted, but the room they were in was cold and bare, empty except for the tall cupboards along one wall and a tin bath in the middle.

Mrs Scrimshaw pulled a pair of scissors from her apron pocket. Without a word she grabbed

Rose by her hair and cut savagely into the long, dark tresses.

'Now, off with your things,' she said, taking a broom and vigorously sweeping the hair into a mound.

Lydia opened her mouth to protest, and then looked at Mrs Scrimshaw. Best not to cross her.

'Give Lucy to me, Rose,' she said. 'You go first.'

'Whose bastard is it?' asked Mrs Scrimshaw.

'Lucy is Rose's babby,' said Lydia, gently taking the child from her daughter.

Rose removed her cracked boots and thin, worn garments. She rolled everything into a bundle, holding it in front of her as she stood, head down, waiting, shivering bare-foot on the cold stone floor.

'Put them mucky old things down there,' Mrs Scrimshaw said. 'I'll burn 'em later. Now get in that bath, and wash yourself and wash your hair.'

The water was murky and soupy. *How many*

others had washed in it? Rose wondered. Mrs Scrimshaw waited, a bar of carbolic soap in one hand and a scrubbing brush in the other.

'Come on. Come on. I haven't got all night,' she said.

Rose bit her lip and tentatively put one foot into the water.

'Get in, and mind you wash yourself properly.' Mrs Scrimshaw handed over the soap and scrubbing brush. 'We don't want any disease here.'

Rose shivered as she climbed into the bath. She lathered the soap over her thin body and cropped hair. Then splashed herself all over with the cold water. While Rose dried herself on a damp grey cloth, Mrs Scrimshaw fetched clothes and boots from the cupboard. She gave a bundle to Rose and a bundle to Lydia. The coarse material was rough to the skin, but at least it would be warm.

'And you're to wear this as well.' She handed Rose a jacket of the same cloth.

'Why?'

'You're a jacket woman.'

'What do you mean?' Lydia asked.

'It's her mark of shame. She's got a bastard child. She'll go to the ward with all the other jacket women.'

'But we want to be together as a family,' Lydia said. 'You're a woman. You must understand that?'

'I understand the law, and the law says families don't stay together. Inmates are to be segregated,' Mrs Scrimshaw said. 'There are separate wards for women, men, girls, boys, jacket women. You're paupers. What d'you expect? Now, Missus, give that babby here while you get in that bath.'

'No!' Rose took the baby from her mother. 'I'll see to Lucy.'

Mrs Scrimshaw turned back to the cupboard

to find baby clothes. Rose gently unrolled the cloths that Lucy was wrapped in, and as she did so removed a small object, like a thin tube. She slipped this into her jacket pocket. Lucy began to whimper as she lay in Rose's arms.

'Please ... Mrs Scrimshaw ... ' Rose asked, 'could I have a little water and a clean cloth so I can wash Lucy on my lap?'

Impatiently Mrs Scrimshaw ripped off a strip of clean linen from a stack in the cupboard and slopped water from a chipped enamel jug into a bowl. Lydia quickly undressed, washed herself in the tin bath, dried herself and dressed, while Rose bathed and dressed Lucy. Then Mrs Scrimshaw locked the cupboards, rattling each door in turn to make sure it was securely fastened.

'I'll take you to your beds now,' she said. 'You've missed supper, but it won't be long till morning.'

Two

A bell was ringing. Tom woke. His whole body was sore. The rough material of his shirt and trousers scraped against his skin, raw from Scrimshaw's brutal scrubbing last night. The straw mattress was lumpy but it was dry, better than the ditch they'd slept in the night before.

'Come on, boys. Time to get up.'

It was a man's voice. Scrimshaw? Tom huddled

under the blanket. No, it was a different voice, stern but not so harsh.

Dazed with sleep Tom sat up, swung his legs out of bed and pushed his feet into his boots. In the dim, early-morning light he saw rows of iron bedsteads. Out of every one tumbled at least one boy, sometimes two, even three. Some looked about his age, fourteen. Some could be as young as maybe six or seven. He'd never seen so many boys. There must be near a hundred.

A tall, bearded man seemed to be in charge. Tom followed the rest of the boys, who were forming a ragged line in front of a long table with half a dozen or so tin bowls of water. Each boy splashed cold water over his face and then moved to the end of the table, where there were cloths to dry themselves. Tom followed suit.

When they'd all finished, they followed the tall man down a passage and across a yard. Nobody spoke. Tom paused for a moment to look around.

Where was Mam? And Rose and Lucy? He felt a fist in his back. The boy behind gave him a shove. He stumbled through the doorway into another corridor, and at the end of that into a high-ceilinged room lined with rows of long tables and benches. The room smelt of stale food. Tom's stomach ached with hunger. The tall man said grace, and then everyone scrambled over the benches and began to eat. The room echoed with the tinny clatter of bowls and spoons.

Tom dipped his spoon into the tin bowl. The gruel was barely warm, but he was so hungry he dunked his bread in it, stuffing the soggy mass into his mouth. He scraped and scraped the bowl with his spoon.

Only then did he look around. The room was full of men and boys, all dressed like him. Most of the men were old or infirm. There were just a few younger ones, unkempt, in shabby, dirty clothes. He knew what they were. Tramps, or vagrants. Everybody looked down on them.

'Where are the women and girls?' he asked the boy next to him. The boy shook his head, placed a finger on his lips.

The clatter of spoons and bowls gradually stopped. The tall man said grace again. Benches scraped back. Nailed boots rasped on the stone floor.

As they left the dining-hall Tom saw a line of women, girls and young children coming towards him. He searched their faces. They all looked the same, with cropped hair and drab clothing. Then he saw Rose, carrying Lucy.

'Rose!'

'Tom!' She reached out a hand and pulled him to one side. 'What happened to you last night?'

'That Porter, Scrimshaw. He burnt my clothes and he scrubbed me till it hurt.' Tom pulled up his sleeve and showed the red-raw skin.

'Oh, Tom!' Rose covered her mouth with her

hand, tears in her dark brown eyes.

'Stop!' The line halted suddenly. The tall man wheeled round and stalked back to where Tom and Rose huddled together.

'Silence!' he said. 'What do you think you're doing? Association between male and female inmates is strictly forbidden.'

'But he's my brother, sir,' Rose said.

'Family members live separately, as you very well know. Any more talking and I'll report you to the Master. Come on. There's work to be done.'

Rose squeezed Tom's hand and then moved back into line. Tom followed the other boys and men out into the yard. The tall man led the younger boys away.

'Where are they going?' Tom asked the boy in front of him.

'School.'

'Who's he?' asked Tom, nodding towards the tall man.

'Mr Henley. Schoolmaster.'

Tom followed the older lads and the men through a large gateway.

'Where are we going, then?' he asked the boy, afraid he was leaving the workhouse and would never see his mother, Rose or Lucy again.

'Farm.'

'What's your name?'

'Alfred.'

'Mine's Tom.'

Alfred didn't reply. He was a boy of few words.

They were set to work mucking out the stables, cowsheds and pigsties. It was bitterly cold. Soon Tom's hands and feet were numb.

In the distance a bell rang.

'Dinner,' said Alfred.

Tom couldn't believe it was only midday. He'd thought it must soon be supper time. His back and shoulders ached with lifting forkfuls of manure and straw. Already his hands were blistered.

The relief of being inside for an hour didn't last. As his hands and feet thawed out, the pain in them was intense, a hot ache. He could hardly bear to hold the knife to cut his bread and cheese. The rule of silence was a blessing. He was too tired to speak.

Then it was outside again, tramping up and down the field, picking taties out of the heavy, wet soil. As the afternoon wore on, clods of earth stuck to his boots, weighing them down. The basket was heavy, the handle slippery with mud, sliding out of the grasp of his numbed fingers. Dusk fell. Tom stumbled on, bent like an old man.

In the darkness the wavering line of men and boys made its way back to the workhouse. Bread and cheese again. But that was better than nothing. The ache in his stomach wasn't so bad. And then bed. At least he was fed and dry, even if he wasn't warm. But his heart ached for Mam and Rose and Lucy. What was happening to them? Where were they? Would they ever be together again?

Three

After Rose had seen Tom that morning on his way from the dining-hall, she looked out for her mother. The line of women and girls gradually moved forward towards the dining-hall door. Rose was almost there when she saw Lydia in the queue behind her. She had to speak to her. She glanced round quickly. She couldn't see either of the Scrimshaws, or the tall man who'd shouted at her and Tom. She slipped out of her place to join her mother. In a whisper she told her what Tom had said about the Porter's cruel treatment of him.

'Poor Tom.' Lydia shook her head.

'Silence, please.'

A youngish woman in a plain, grey dress was standing at the entrance to the dining-hall. Like Mrs Scrimshaw, she had a bunch of keys at her waist, but her voice, although firm, was pleasant.

She's not so bad, Rose thought. *She did say please.*

After breakfast they filed out into the yard.

'Now you children go with Miss Todd,' Mrs Scrimshaw said, and the younger woman set off with the little ones trotting behind her. The older girls and the women waited to receive their orders for the day.

'You can do two hours in the dairy,' Mrs Scrimshaw pointed at Lydia, 'and then you're both to go before the Board of Guardians.'

Lydia nodded. She'd never been inside a workhouse before, but she knew poor people had to prove to rich people that they needed shelter. The Board must be the rich people: farmers and such.

'Go on, follow them.' Mrs Scrimshaw jerked her head towards the group of women going through the main gateway.

Lydia squeezed Rose's hand and hurried off.

'And, as for you,' Mrs Scrimshaw frowned at Rose, 'you're in the laundry.'

'Can't I go to the dairy with my mam?' Rose asked.

'Certainly not. Just you come along with me, and do as you're told. You've far too much to say for yourself, my gel.'

Rose followed. She was worried about Lucy, who was hungry and fretful. She'd seen that morning that the mothers in the jacketers' ward smuggled food in for the babies and younger children. But Harriet, another young mother, had told Rose that there was never enough food. Harriet said Mrs Scrimshaw regularly raided the cupboards in the jacketers' ward, throwing away every scrap of food she found. So then they had to start hoarding all over again.

A stout woman in a black, silk dress showed Lydia and Rose into the Board room. They'd never been in such a grand room before. It was panelled in dark wood. A bright fire burned in a handsome fireplace. Six men sat round a long, polished table.

'Thank you, Matron,' said the man seated at the top of the table.

'Mr Birch.' She bowed her head and rustled out of the room.

Lydia and Rose waited.

This must be the Board, thought Lydia, observing the six men in their dark clothes. Five of them wore gold watch chains looped across their waistcoats. The sixth had no watch chain, but wore one of those white bands round his neck. *He'd be the Parson*, she thought.

The fire crackled, chairs creaked, Lucy murmured. Rose hushed her. Mr Birch glanced at the black marble clock on the mantelpiece.

'Right,' he said. 'We'll start now. The boy's working on the farm, so we won't take him away from his labours. We can't afford to lose a single pair of hands at this time of year, can we, Mr Grey?'

'That's right,' said a stout, red-faced man. 'You want to get those taties lifted before the frosts.'

Mr Birch, looking sternly at Lydia and Rose, began to question them. So many questions:

'Surname? ... Christian name? ... Address? ... Place and date of birth? ... Religion?'

The man on Mr Birch's left wrote down their answers in a large leather-bound book, pausing from time to time to dip his pen into a silver inkwell.

Finally, the question, 'So why do you need indoor relief?'

Mr Birch leant forward as Lydia responded in barely a whisper. Rose studied the tips of her boots.

Then Mr Birch summarised Lydia's reply, speaking slowly so that the man on his left could write it all down.

'Mother and children deserted, father's whereabouts unknown, no other living relatives. Boy, fourteen, labourer; sixteen-year-old girl with illegitimate child of ten months.' He paused. 'So, what do you think, gentlemen?'

There were murmurs around the table, shaking of heads.

What will we do? thought Rose. *Where will we go*

if they won't let us stay here? We'll starve. Anything's better than that.

'Yes, Mr Grey?' enquired Mr Birch of the stout, red-faced man.

Glancing at Rose and her baby, Mr Grey spoke in a low voice to the men sitting on either side of him. They nodded their heads. Other heads began to nod too.

'All agreed? Right,' Mr Birch said, 'if you could note this in the Register, Mr Wainwright – Lydia, Rose, Thomas and Lucy Maddison, admitted to the Union Workhouse, 18 November 1838. That will be all, gentlemen.'

The men rose from the table and gathered around the fire. Mr Grey paused to bend over the sleeping baby in Rose's arms. He smiled. Rose looked up at him gratefully, but he'd already moved quickly away to join the other gentlemen.

Four

Rose saved her bread at dinner and supper, and at breakfast the next day. She slipped the pieces into her pocket. Although Tom was wiry like his father, he was small and slight. How would he manage the long hours working in the fields? Meals here were regular, but the helpings were small. If they'd been together as a family, she could have given him some of her share, but they didn't even meet at meal-times.

However, she had a plan. She'd noticed that the exercise yard for the boys adjoined the women's yard where they hung out the washing. Yesterday, behind the high wall, she'd heard voices and the tramp, tramp of heavy boots.

At this time of year the women hated going out into the yard to hang out the wet linen or fetch it in, especially when there was a frost, like today, and the sheets hung stiff on the line. They'd rather stay in the steamy atmosphere of the laundry room. So Rose offered to carry out the heavy basket of wet sheets, knowing that nobody would object.

The ground was so hard this morning, with the frost, that the labourers had been sent back early for dinner. They were in the next yard, whiling away the time until twelve. Rose could hear their voices, and amongst them Tom's. As she slowly pegged the sodden sheets out on the line, she studied the wall separating the two yards. It was so high. How could she let Tom know she was here and had food for him?

She looked over her shoulder to see if anyone was watching from the laundry room. Thank goodness, the windows were all steamed up. Nobody could see her.

She went closer to the wall. In places the brickwork was worn and irregular. About two feet up some bricks jutted out from the others, as if they'd loosened, forming a kind of ledge. If she could get a toehold on those and grab the top edge of the wall, she could lean over, attract Tom's attention and then throw him the bread. She took it out of her pocket. It was all ready, tied in a clean rag.

She looked around again to make sure no one was watching her, took a run, got one foot onto a jutting-out brick, and grasped the top of the wall. She heaved herself up for just long enough to look over, see Tom, call his name and throw the parcel of bread into the yard.

It was done in a moment. She almost fell backwards, but it was worth it to see the delight on Tom's freckled face.

'And what do you think you're doing, Maddison?'

It was Mrs Scrimshaw.

'Come with me, straight to the Master. We'll see what Mr Clements has to say about this.'

Now what had she done? Her satisfaction in Tom's pleasure had hardly lasted a minute. What if she and Lucy were sent away? If they were, they'd surely starve to death.

She recognised the Master. He'd been in the Board room yesterday, next to the man who'd written everything down in the big book. The Matron sat beside him.

'Rose Maddison. Caught throwing bread over the wall to the boys,' announced Mrs Scrimshaw.

'Thank you, Mrs Scrimshaw. You may return to your duties now,' said Mr Clements.

Reluctantly, Mrs Scrimshaw left the room.

'I'm sorry to see you before me so soon,' the Master said.

'I wanted to give my brother some more bread,' Rose explained. 'He's not strong, and he's labouring in the fields all day.'

'I understand your concerns, Maddison, but the diet is adequate. The Poor Law Commissioners have laid it down, and they have your best interests at heart. It's not for you to question their decisions.'

'We can't have bits of food lying about the yards,' the Matron added. 'You must understand that. It would encourage rats and disease. You wouldn't want that for your baby, would you?'

'We have to make an example of you,' the

Master said. 'This isn't the first time, is it Maddison?'

'I've never done that before.' Rose tried to keep the indignation out of her voice.

'No,' the Master said, 'but on your first morning here you broke one of our rules. I understand from Mr Henley, the schoolmaster, that he had cause to reprimand you and your brother for talking together outside the dining-hall.'

Rose could feel her heart thudding. She rubbed her sweaty palms down the front of her calico pinafore. Please God he wouldn't take Lucy from her.

Rose looked from the Master to the Matron.

'Twelve hours in the Refractory Cell, I think,' the Master said.

'A cell, sir. Please don't send me to prison, sir. I can't leave my babby.'

'It's not prison, Maddison,' the Matron said. 'It's the Punishment Cell here, in the workhouse.'

'For any inmate who breaks the rules,' the Master added.

'I wonder, Mr Clements,' the Matron said, 'whether we should reduce the hours of imprisonment since Maddison has a young infant to care for?'

The Master frowned.

'Very well, Mrs Clements,' he said, 'but do not take advantage of our leniency, Maddison.'

'No, sir.'

The Master opened a drawer in his desk, took out a small, black leather-bound book and began to write. Rose waited. Then he read out what he'd written.

'Eight hours in total tomorrow in the Refractory Cell, from eight to twelve and from one to five. Boiled rice for every meal instead of the prescribed diet for the day.'

He rose from his chair and looked sternly at Rose.

'Remember, Maddison, anyone here who commits an offence may be sent before a Magistrate and sentenced to a term in prison, if the offence is sufficiently serious. I hope you will not come to my attention again.'

He opened the door.

'Mrs Scrimshaw.'

She appeared at once.

'Take Maddison back to the laundry, and ask Mr Scrimshaw to bring Tom Maddison here immediately.'

It's all my fault, thought Rose. *I meant to help Tom, but I've only got him into trouble.*

Five

Tom stood before the Master's desk, his head down, turning his cap in his hands.

'It's a serious offence,' the Master said. 'Rose Maddison broke the rules by throwing her bread over the wall, and you committed an equally serious offence by taking it and eating it. In fact the greater offence in my opinion. I have to make an example of you both. I've been considering whether I should send you before the Magistrate.'

Tom looked up quickly. They were going to send him to prison. The shame of it would kill his mother.

You have to be punished, Maddison, and you must take your punishment like a man.'

'I will, sir,' Tom said earnestly.

The Master was silent for several minutes.

Then he picked up his pen and wrote in the Punishment Book.

'Tomorrow morning,' he said, 'you will pump water for three hours continuously. You will have only boiled rice to eat. In the afternoon you will pick oakum.'

'Yes, sir. Thank you, sir.'

He was relieved not to go before the Magistrate and face a certain prison sentence, but he knew his punishment was not a light one. Only yesterday, the Master had announced that all able-bodied men in the workhouse should undertake the task of pumping water for three or four hours at a time. The men knew very well that the Workhouse Guardians thought they were all lazy good-for-nothings, and that they hoped to discourage them from staying in the workhouse by giving them this exhausting and back-breaking task. Likewise, everyone hated oakum-picking; it was a tedious job, and so hard on the fingers that they bled.

'There's no light in there at all,' Harriet told Rose. 'It's like a dungeon. I should know! First week I was here I got sent to the Punishment Cell for dancing in the front yard with another jacket woman, and swearing at Ma Scrimshaw when she told us to stop. It was terrible in that cell, dark and cold.'

Rose shuddered.

'But it were worth it,' Harriet laughed, 'to see the look on her face when I told her where to go! It didn't stop me swearing though. I just do it under my breath now so she don't hear!'

Rose laughed too, in spite of herself.

That evening, Rose managed to speak to her mother as they left the dining-hall, and warn her that she wouldn't see her the next day.

'I'll be all right,' she whispered. 'I'll be back on the ward tomorrow night. It's not so bad, and at least Tom got his extra bread.'

She tried to smile.

But when she lay in bed that night she wondered, *What kind of place is this, where families are kept apart, and a simple act of kindness is punished?*

The next day Mrs Scrimshaw escorted Rose from the ward, along empty corridors and down a flight of steps to the Punishment Cell, below ground. She unlocked the door with a huge key and pushed it open. Rose just had time to see bare walls, glistening with damp, a straw mattress on the floor and a wooden bench by the wall. Then the heavy door was shut and bolted.

Thick darkness pressed against her eyes. She gasped in panic. She couldn't see. She couldn't breathe. She reached out where she thought the bench should be. There was nothing there. She slid one foot forward, then the other, hands outstretched. Still nothing. She must try again. The cell was small. If she kept moving forward she must find the bench. She took another tiny step and another. Then hit the edge of the bench with her knee, and fell forward onto it.

She pulled her feet up onto the bench and sat

with her arms clasped round her knees. She had to keep her feet off the floor. There might be rats. The bench was hard. The mattress might be more comfortable, but she wasn't going to lie on that. She shuddered at the thought of some creature scuttling over her face as she lay asleep. And the mattress was probably full of lice anyway. She strained her ears for any sounds, but there was nothing except the hiss of silence in her ears.

She had no way of knowing how much time had passed. She only knew she was getting colder and the bench was getting harder. A damp, musty smell filled her nostrils. She longed to stretch out and sleep, but she must stay awake. She stared into the darkness.

She must have dozed though, for she thought she heard Lucy crying. When she woke she was leaning her head against the wall, the gritty surface pressing into her cheek. Then she heard sounds outside the door. Someone was turning the key, sliding back the bolts. It must be Mrs Scrimshaw.

But it wasn't. It was Miss Todd.

'Come along, my dear.' She took Rose's arm, helping her up off the bench. 'I've come to take you for your dinner. Mrs Scrimshaw is busy admitting two new inmates. My goodness, you can barely stand.'

'Lucy,' said Rose, 'I must see Lucy.'

'She's on the ward,' said Miss Todd, 'Jepson is looking after her. You shall go and see her first.'

After her dinner of plain boiled rice, Rose was handed back into the charge of Mrs Scrimshaw, and Miss Todd returned to the school-room. Rose looked out for Tom in the corridor, but there was no sign of him. It was so hard to be locked away again. She dreaded the bitter cold, but she was sure now that there were no rats, and she knew the time would pass, however slowly.

And while Rose endured the cold and dark of an underground prison, Tom pumped water, until his hands were shaking and his arms and back ached with the continuous effort. After three hours of non-stop pumping, he could barely stand.

'Lean on me, mate,' said Alfred.

In the dining-hall Tom sat apart from the others to eat his boiled rice. His hands quivered so much that the spoon shook as he lifted it to his mouth, and the rice fell off, back into the basin. Before he'd managed to eat even two mouthfuls, Scrimshaw appeared behind him and grabbed him by the collar.

'Maddison! Get up, boy. It's time you joined the oakum-pickers. You'll enjoy that!' He laughed harshly.

Tom staggered as he tried to stand, knocking the bench over.

'Watch what you're doing, you young oaf,' Scrimshaw shouted.

Tom tried to lift the bench back into position, but dropped it with a clatter on the stone floor.

'Leave it, mate, I'll do it.' It was Alfred.

'Get back to your place, Kemp!' shouted Scrimshaw.

He turned to Tom, 'Now, you put that bench back. And you stay where you are, Kemp. He shall do it himself, with help from nobody.'

Somehow Tom managed to lift the heavy bench. Then, head down, he followed Scrimshaw out of the dining-hall. He hoped he might catch a glimpse of Rose on the way to the workroom, but she was nowhere to be seen.

The overseer dumped a pile of old hemp ropes in front of Tom.

'Get them unpicked, boy,' he said.

All through the afternoon in the cold, dim room, Tom bent over the thick rope, untwisting and separating the strands, until his fingernails broke and the hemp was stained with his blood.

Back on the ward Alfred bound Tom's fingers with bits of rag, and then Tom lay down on his mattress and tried to sleep. But, half-dreaming, half-waking, his arms seemed to be moving up and down, up and down, as he worked at the pump, and his fingers endlessly seemed to be untwisting fibres of rope which twisted together again before he could finish. And so on and so on ...

Six

The days and weeks passed. It was as if there had never been a life outside the workhouse, as a family, with their father, in their own home.

The food was monotonous – bread and gruel, bread and cheese. But on Mondays there was broth for dinner. On Thursdays, they had suet pudding with vegetables, and on Sundays there was *meat* pudding with vegetables.

Tom's stomach rumbled on Sunday mornings

when the smell of beef or mutton meat wafted down the corridors. He savoured the meat, holding each piece in his mouth, sucking out the flavour. He knew that the women were given two ounces less than the men. He was proud to have a man's portion, but wished he could sometimes give it to his mother and his sister when he saw them on Sunday afternoons. Yet, remembering what happened when Rose threw him her portion of bread, he dare not break the rules. And he knew that they still ate more meat now than they ever did when they lived at home. There was never enough, but it was regular.

So, despite the hard work and the long hours, they all grew stronger. They went to bed, exhausted, at eight and they were still tired out when they rose at quarter to seven, but they were all healthier than they'd been in a very long time.

All, that is, except Lucy, who didn't thrive. She was a fretful baby. The other mothers complained she kept everyone awake at night with her crying.

'She's a mawngy one,' Rachel said.

'She's faddy,' Martha said. 'I wouldn't give in to her.'

Rose sat on her bed in the dark ward, rocking Lucy. Everyone else was asleep. She felt so alone, trying to quieten Lucy in whispers. She was worn out from the long day in the laundry, scrubbing the men's rough shirts, wringing out heavy, wet sheets. Every so often her head drooped. Then she jerked awake, and held Lucy more tightly. She could have dropped her. She mustn't fall asleep.

In the early hours of the morning, Lucy's breathing became more regular and she finally slept, and Rose herself could sleep too.

It seemed to Rose that the getting-up bell rang as soon as she lay down. She dragged herself up out of a deep sleep and woke Lucy, who immediately started crying again. *If only we had our own home*, thought Rose despairingly. *If only Mam were near at hand.*

It was the middle of December, and the days were getting even shorter. Every morning was bitterly cold, the ground hard with frost. Lydia, Rose and Tom had chilblains on their feet and hands. There was no relief from the constant itching. Tom had blisters as well, from pulling turnips up out of the frozen ground. It was one long round of hard work and physical pain. Everyone was in low spirits.

Then one day in the laundry Rose overheard the other women talking.

'I heard Matron telling Ma Scrimshaw,' Amy said, 'that the Guardians've decided we're to have roast beef and taties on Christmas Day ... '

' ... and plum puddin' ... ' said Sophie.

'We women are to have tea, sugar, butter and snuff!' Amy added.

'What about the men and the bairns?' Hannah asked.

'Ale and 'baccy for the men, and oranges and nuts for the bairns!' Amy said triumphantly.

The women clapped their hands with delight. Rose beamed with pleasure. This was something to look forward to.

But her pleasure didn't last long. A few days later, after Sunday dinner, the Master rose from the top table.

'The Guardians have asked me to remind you,' he said, 'that Christmas Dinner is a privilege, and as such will be enjoyed only by those who deserve it. Therefore able-bodied men are excluded from Christmas dinner ... '

He paused and looked down the long tables to where the jacket women sat with their babies and the younger children. Rose felt he was staring just at her. She rested her chin on the top of Lucy's head.

The Master continued, 'And the jacket women are also excluded, on account of their immorality.'

'No!'

Rose couldn't stop herself.

'Silence!' the Master roared.

Rose felt her face go hot. He was looking straight at her. He knew she was the one who cried out. She glanced round the table at the other women. Many looked sullen, defeated. Others were in tears. Some, she could tell, were full of rage, like her, but trying their best to hide it.

She went straight from the dining-hall to the Day Ward to spend an hour or two with her mother and Tom. They all looked forward to that time, just once a week, when they could be together as a family.

'If the jacket women's children don't get Christmas Dinner either, it's not right,' said Rose. 'I know Lucy's too young to realise. But there are near thirty children in my ward, and twenty or more are old enough to understand. Why should they suffer? Do you think we should speak to the Master?'

'Yes, I do,' Lydia said, 'and I think we should do it now. It's Sunday after all. What's it they say? The better the day, the better the deed. He's stern, but I think he's fair.'

'Go and see him now?' Rose asked, suddenly afraid.

'Yes, now,' said Lydia, 'while our courage is up.'

Rose got up slowly, remembering the scene in the Master's office after she'd thrown the bread over the wall to Tom. He'd made an example of her then for breaking the rules. Would he punish her again for shouting out at dinner, and now daring to question his authority? *But whatever he might do*, she thought, *she must still say her piece.*

'All right,' she said, 'maybe he will be kinder after going to chapel this morning. Tom, can you look after Lucy while we're gone?'

Scrimshaw opened the door of the Master's office.

'What d'you want?'

'We want to speak to the Master, sir,' Lydia said.

'It's Sunday a'ternoon. He's in his parlour. You can see him tomorrow.'

'We need to see him now,' Rose said.

'You'll just 'ave ter wait,' said Scrimshaw.

At that moment they heard heavy footsteps behind them. It was the Master.

'What's this, Scrimshaw?'

'They want to see you, sir, but I've told 'em. They'll 'ave to wait till mornin'.'

'That won't be necessary, Scrimshaw. I'll see them now. Go back to the Lodge.'

Scrimshaw turned away, scowling at Rose and Lydia over his shoulder.

'Well?' the Master asked.

'It's the jacket women's children, sir,' Rose said in a rush of words. 'Not the babbies, but those old enough to understand. Will they miss Christmas Dinner as well, and not get nuts and oranges like the other bairns?'

'Indeed they *will* miss Christmas Dinner, as they will remain in the care of their mothers, as is right and proper.'

'But it's not fair, sir.' Rose's heart beat faster, but she didn't falter. 'It's not their fault they're bastards.'

When she finished speaking she could feel herself trembling. She'd said too much. The Master was frowning. He'd send her to the Punishment Cell again. Who'd look after Lucy then?

'I'll talk to the Guardians tomorrow,' he said eventually, 'and see what they think. I can't say more than that.'

Both Rose and Lydia spent a restless night, worried they'd gone too far.

True to his word though, the Master spoke to the Guardians. At supper that night Miss Todd, the schoolmistress, who was supervising the meal, announced the Board's decision.

'Every child in the workhouse, except the babies, but including the jacketers' children, will have Christmas Dinner, followed by nuts and oranges.'

There was great rejoicing in the jacketers' ward that night. The women crowded round Rose. Harriet kissed her, and even Martha and Rachel smiled at her. For the first time, Rose felt she belonged. She wasn't ashamed to be a jacket woman, whatever Mrs Scrimshaw said. She knew how much she and the other women loved their children.

On Christmas Day the jacketers had to stay in their ward from after breakfast until supper. Mrs Scrimshaw brought dinner in, helped by two of the women. It was the usual Friday diet, six ounces of bread and three-quarters of an ounce of butter each. It was a poor meal for Christmas Day, but they comforted themselves, imagining their children enjoying a proper Christmas Dinner.

'They'll be tucking in now to beef and taties,' said Sophie. She licked her lips. 'Just think of that lovely gravy!'

'My Davy'll be licking his plate clean,' Amy laughed. 'I hope old Scrimshaw don't see him!'

'I'm sure I can smell the pudding,' Harriet said.

'My Emily's never had plum pudding. And she's never seen an orange, let alone ate one.'

When the children came back onto the ward, their hands and faces were sticky with plum pudding and orange juice. The women laughed as they kissed them.

'Mmm!' Harriet hugged Emily. 'I can taste the plum pudding now! Here, Rose, you have a taste. It's thanks to you they've had a proper Christmas Dinner,' and she gently pushed her six-year-old towards Rose.

Rose kissed Emily. This comradeship was a kind of family too.

Seven

As the weeks went by, Rose became more worried about Lucy. Instead of gaining in weight and strength, the child seemed lighter, almost shrunken. During the day, whilst Rose worked, she lay passively for hours. At night she cried and tossed and turned. Rose couldn't pacify her.

By Sunday afternoon Rose was consumed with anxiety. She wept as she gave Lucy to Lydia to hold, and saw her own fear in her mother's face.

'We'll ask Matron to call in the Medical Officer if she's no better by tomorrow morning,' Lydia said.

When Dr Lowe examined Lucy he could find nothing wrong. There were no signs of cholera or scarlet fever. He recommended extra bread and milk, and that Rose take Lucy for an airing every afternoon in the yard, when the weather was fine.

Rose and Lydia were reassured, and over the next few weeks Lucy's health seemed to improve. But then several of the children on the ward developed a nasty cough, and Lucy was among them. The others recovered after a few days, but Lucy couldn't shake it off. Some of the other mothers, Martha and Rachel in particular, complained that she was disturbing everyone's sleep, and so once again Rose felt the outsider.

One Saturday night she was feeling especially low. Lucy just wouldn't settle. The ward was quiet and everyone else was asleep, but Lucy was whimpering. Rose tried to shush her. Her whimpers became wails. Other children stirred. One child started coughing, and then another.

'Shut that babby up!' shouted the woman in the next bed.

'I'm sorry, Judith,' Rose said, 'but I can't.'

'You're useless!' Judith pulled the blanket over her head.

Rose began to cry, her sobs mingling with Lucy's. She was so tired. Judith was right. She was useless. Any of the other mothers could soothe their children to sleep.

'Rose.'

It was Elizabeth, the woman from the bed opposite. She'd three children under seven with her on the ward, and another, a boy of eight, in the boys' ward. She was a confident mother, noisy and cheerful.

'This is the best thing for her,' she said, coming over to stand by Rose's bed, holding a small dark brown bottle. 'Laudanum. It's always worked with mine. It'll give her and you a good night's rest, and that'll shut *her* up too,' she added, nodding towards Judith. 'Just give Lucy a spoonful with a little sugar.'

Rose sat up and took the bottle and the sugar in its twist of paper.

'Thank you.'

Elizabeth returned to her bed, and Rose crept over to the cupboard to find a basin and spoon. By the moonlight shining through the tall window she could see well enough to mix a spoonful of laudanum and a sprinkle of sugar. Lucy didn't want to take the mixture. She squirmed and wriggled in Rose's arms, turning her head from side to side.

'Please, please, Lucy,' whispered Rose.

Eventually the spoon was empty. Rose lay Lucy down beside her. Gradually she quietened and her breathing became regular, and Rose also fell asleep.

During the night Rose woke. Lucy's breathing was slower, irregular. Her skin felt cold and clammy. *There must be a really hard frost*, thought Rose sleepily. She cuddled Lucy against her. The child stirred slightly. Rose drifted back into sleep.

When she woke again it was morning. In the dim light Rose could see Lucy as she lay beside her in the bed. She was lying on her back, apparently awake but not crying. As Rose bent to pick her up, she noticed Lucy's eyes were strange, staring, the pupils tiny pinpoints. Her skin was as cold as stone.

By early afternoon Lucy's body had been

examined by Dr Lowe and then removed to the Mortuary. Lydia, Tom and Rose huddled together in a corner of the Day Ward, keeping as far away as they could from the other families who were enjoying their Sunday afternoon reunion. They sat without speaking, their heads bowed.

Lydia blamed herself for bringing her children to the workhouse in the first place. This would never have happened if they hadn't come here. Tom wished desperately that he could think of something to say to Rose that would comfort her. Rose tormented herself for giving Lucy the laudanum. Why? Why had she done that?

'I forced her to take it,' she said. 'She didn't like it. But I made her, just because I was tired and afraid of the others.'

Lydia tried to reassure her.

'I've given all of you laudanum,' she said, 'and nothing went awry with that. But I've lost babies as well, three in all, and so've most women I know, especially poor folk like us. Don't blame yourself, my love. You were a loving mother to that babby. She never went short of love.'

She put her arms round Rose and held her close.

Eight

As Tom and Rose walked back to their separate wards at the end of the afternoon, Mrs Scrimshaw appeared.

'You're to go before the Board tomorrow afternoon, Maddison,' she said to Rose. 'You're going to be in trouble, my gel.'

Rose watched her stalk away down the corridor.

'Tom, what shall I do? They think it was my

fault Lucy died. They'll send me to prison. I'll never see you or Mam again.'

Tom put his arm round her shoulders.

'There's something I've got to tell you, Rose,' he said, 'but I couldn't in front of our mam. A tramp came in last Thursday night, and he worked alongside me on Friday. When we walked up the field for dinner, he started playing a tune on a reed whistle. And do you know what, Rose, the whistle was one of father's!'

'Are you sure?' Rose rubbed her eyes with the back of her hand.

'Almost. Have you still got the one father made you?'

'Yes. I hid it in Lucy's clothes before we came here. And then ... before they took her to the Mortuary I hid it in my pocket.'

She took it out and gave it to Tom. He turned it over in his hand.

'I remember our dad making this,' he said. 'Do you?'

'Of course I do. He was sitting by the grate, whittling away with his old knife, and Mam said – *Samuel Maddison, stop making that mess on my hearth!*'

Tom examined the whistle.

'The tramp's was just like this. I'm sure it was made by our dad.'

'Where'd he get it?'

'Said a man gave it him at Broughton Union.'

'That's more than twenty miles away!'

'Yes. He said he travels all over, a night here, a night there.'

'Did he know the man's name?'

'No. He said he never gives his own name, and never asks other people's. Keeps himself to himself. But the man he met said he was looking for work, and that he wanted to be back with his family.'

‘Oh, Tom, if it’s really our dad ... ’

‘We must go and see, just in case it is.’

‘But I can’t leave, Lucy ... I know she’s gone, but ... ’

‘It’s all right. I can go on my own.’

‘Can’t we wait till after Lucy’s buried?’

‘We should go straightaway. If it was Dad at Broughton, he might have moved on before we got there. This is our best chance.’

‘I don’t know what to do. But you can’t go alone. It’s not safe ... I’ll come with you.’

‘I can look after myself.’

‘I can’t let you go on your own. I’ve lost Lucy. I couldn’t bear to lose you as well. I’ll come with you, as long as we’re back before the burial.’

‘We’ll go tomorrow morning. Let’s meet behind the hay store as soon as we can get away. If you’re there first, just wait for me.’

‘All right. At least it’s something to hope for.’

‘But we mustn’t get our hopes up too much.’

Next morning, Rose took the clean linen for the Master and Matron from the laundry across to their own quarters. But afterwards, instead of going back to the laundry, she slipped out of a side-gate and went round to the back of the hay store where Tom was already waiting.

Rose hid the empty laundry basket in some bushes, while Tom kept watch.

'Best go across the fields,' Tom said. 'Can you jump that ditch?'

'Of course I can.' Rose lifted her skirts and leapt across into the next field. Tom followed. Bending down, they scurried along the edge of the field, taking what cover they could from the hedgerow. They climbed a gate into the next field, crossed another ditch and then scrambled through the hedge into a muddy lane. They walked at a steady pace, pausing only for a few minutes to eat the bread and cheese they'd saved from the previous night's supper. They'd keep their breakfast bread for later.

After a while they cut across a field and came out into a lane. They weren't sure which way to go, and decided to turn left. But after several hundred yards they came across a milestone, and realised they were going in the wrong direction. They retraced their steps, and were just back on the right road when they heard the clatter of a horse and cart behind them.

'Quick, let's hide down here! It might be someone from Fenbridge!' Tom pushed his way through the bushes at the side of the road and jumped into the ditch. The water came above his boots.

'Oh, Tom, I can't,' Rose said.

'You've got to. Hurry! It'll be round the bend in a minute and they'll see you.'

He grabbed her hand and Rose slid down the

grassy bank, catching her skirt on the brambles. They ducked down in the bottom of the ditch. Rose felt the water seeping through her thin boots. She held her breath as the horse and cart rattled closer.

There was a scrabbling noise in the bushes at the top of the bank. A dog, sniffing and scratching at the earth. Tom felt Rose's nails digging into his hand as she tightened her grip. They kept absolutely still, although their legs ached from crouching.

'Whoa! Whoa!' shouted a rough voice. It was the driver of the horse and cart, but not a voice they recognised.

The horse neighed. The cart stopped.

What if the dog picked up their scent? Or the man got off the cart and followed the dog? He'd be sure to see them.

'Come 'ere, y'old varmint,' he shouted.

The dog clawed frantically at the ground. *It*

must be after a more interesting smell than ours, thought Rose. *Maybe rabbits?* Her nose itched. She'd have to scratch it any minute now. And her feet were freezing.

There was a sudden roar of rage. The dog realised its master had had enough. It spun round, showering soil all over Tom, and then disappeared from view.

'Gee-up!' the man called, and the wheels began to rumble as the cart gathered speed.

Tom and Rose waited until the sound of wheels and hooves had faded away, then they scrambled up the slope and onto the road.

'I'm so stiff,' Rose said. 'My feet are soaked and my skirt's all wet and muddy.'

She gathered it up and wrung out as much of the water as she could.

'Come on,' Tom said. 'We'd better get going.'

Rose shook out the folds of her skirt and pushed back her hair, smearing her face with mud.

'You don't half look a sight,' Tom laughed.

'I expect I do,' said Rose with a little smile. 'But you don't look any better! You're covered in muck!'

For the rest of the day they were lucky. The narrow lanes were deserted and they made good progress, relying on milestones and finger posts to keep them going in the right direction.

At times they both realised they were almost enjoying it – the freedom and the fresh air. The hedges were just beginning to come into bud and the birds were busy. But then they'd wonder how long it would be before someone noticed they were missing. Would they be followed? They tried to comfort themselves by remembering that at least the tramp had already left the workhouse. He couldn't be questioned if anyone suspected he might know where they'd gone. But what would their mother think? What would the Board of Governors do when Rose didn't appear at their meeting? Would they think she'd run away because she was guilty?

Nine

Darkness was falling.

'We must find somewhere to spend the night,' Rose said. 'Maybe we could go and knock at the next cottage we come to and ask if they could let us have a bed for the night, or sleep in an out-house?'

She hated the idea of being outside all through the dark night. She longed for light and warmth and company.

‘No. It wouldn’t be safe. They might have heard someone’s gone missing from Fenbridge Workhouse. Best thing is to look for an old farm building.’

‘I suppose you’re right,’ Rose said, trying hard not to think about rats and foxes.

Luckily it was a dry night and there was a moon. Eventually they saw the dark shape of a building near a bend in the lane. It was a small shed. The door was broken off its hinges, but the roof was intact. Moonlight shone through the open doorway onto a pile of rusting tools in one corner and a stack of wood in another.

Rose stopped in the doorway.

‘What if there are rats, Tom?’

Tom went in, kicked the logs and peered behind the door.

‘It’s all right, Rose. Look, there are sacks here. They’ll keep us warm.’

Rose's feet were cold and sore, and she'd blisters on both heels where her boots had rubbed the skin raw. She was desperate to rest. Reluctantly she went into the hut and sat down on the sack Tom had spread on the ground. She pulled another sack round her shoulders. The sacks were rough and dusty, caked with dried mud and smelling of earth, but they were better than nothing.

Gradually they began to feel a little warmer. They unwrapped the bread they'd kept from breakfast. Tom was hungry and ate his quickly. Rose nibbled hers. It was dry and stale. She wrinkled her nose, and handed the rest to Tom.

'You have this, Tom. I just don't fancy it.'

While Tom munched the last of the bread, Rose gazed through the doorway, trying to remember what life had been like at home, just after Lucy was born, when they'd all been together with their father. It seemed such a long time ago. She couldn't remember it properly. So much had happened since then.

Tom's voice interrupted her thoughts.

'We must leave early,' he said, 'in case anyone comes.'

They slept fitfully. Sometimes when she woke, Rose felt hopeful that the man at Broughton Union would be their father. Then she was convinced it wasn't him, or, if it was, he'd be long gone and they'd never find him. Tom also alternated between hope and despair. He imagined his mother's joy when he told her they'd found their father, and then, more vividly, her shame and sorrow when he and Rose were brought back to the workhouse in disgrace.

They woke next morning cold and hungry. Their clothes were crumpled and grubby, still damp and muddy from their time in the ditch.

Their faces and hands were grimy from the dusty sacks. They'd nothing left to eat, and there were still many miles to go.

As the day wore on they felt sick and light-headed. They hardly spoke, except to decide which direction to take. Once, when they paused to discuss whether to take the right or the left fork in the path, Tom said,

'You look done in, Rose. Shall we rest here for a bit?'

'No. I daren't stop. I might never get up again. We must keep moving.'

At last, in the distance, they saw a large, red brick building, surrounded by high walls. Broughton Union Workhouse.

From the Porter's Lodge they were taken before the Master of the workhouse. Tom was in the middle of telling him about the tramp, the whistle and their father, when the Porter reappeared. He was closely followed by Scrimshaw.

'George Scrimshaw, Porter from Fenbridge Workhouse, Master. He's come for these two. He managed to pick up their trail.'

'Mr Scrimshaw will take you back now,' the Master said. 'You'll be there before dark.'

'But we want to see our father,' Rose protested.

'Some old cock and bull story,' Scrimshaw said, 'and *she's* not to be trusted. Poisoned her own child, she did. Should have been before the Board of Guardians yesterday. All them gentlemen waiting to send her to court. She'll go to prison she will. That's what she deserves.'

'She doesn't!' Tom shouted. 'She didn't poison Lucy.'

Rose felt she had no fight left in her. Everybody believed she'd murdered her own babby. Those rich gentlemen on the Board, that's what they thought. Because she was poor and had a bastard child, they thought she'd no morals, and that she was a bad mother. Only Mam and Tom believed in her, and there was nothing they could do.

Tom rushed at Scrimshaw, who grabbed his wrists, forcing his hands behind his back. Tom kicked and wriggled, but couldn't escape.

'See what I mean,' Scrimshaw said. 'Nothin' but trouble, both of 'em. Have bin all along. I'll take 'em off your hands, sir.'

The Master inclined his head. Then he turned his back as Scrimshaw, holding Rose by the wrist and Tom by the ear, dragged them from the room.

Ten

Samuel Maddison, who'd spent the day stone-breaking with the other tramps, was crossing the yard on his way back to the casuals' ward when he heard a voice he thought he recognised.

'Let go of my sister! Get your hands off her!'

It was his son. Tom!

He watched as a stocky figure pushed two smaller, thinner ones into back of a cart, then jumped up on to the front, picked up the reins and slashed the whip across the horse's back.

Despite his aching limbs and his heavy boots, Samuel started to run after the cart as it rumbled down the drive, gradually gaining speed.

'Stop! Stop! Tom! Rose!' he shouted.

In the fading light he could see the two figures in the back of the cart waving at him, but their voices were so faint he couldn't hear them. The horse was going too fast for him to keep up. He stood, panting, holding his side, as the horse and cart turned into the road and disappeared from sight.

On their return to Fenbridge Tom and Rose were kept under close watch; they were not allowed to speak to anyone.

The following morning they went before the Board.

Rose went in first.

'Now, Maddison, tell us in your own words what happened to your child, Lucy Maddison,' Mr Birch said.

In a low voice Rose described the events of the night before Lucy's death and how she'd woken in the morning to find Lucy dead by her side. The men listened in silence.

'Any questions, gentlemen?' Mr Birch looked round the table.

Rose waited anxiously. Head down. She couldn't meet their eyes. She was afraid of what they thought of her, how they would look at her.

'No? Very well, you may go, Maddison, and wait outside.'

'Thank you, sir.'

Rose wondered why they hadn't asked her any questions. Had they made up their minds already?

Mrs Scrimshaw was waiting outside the door, with Elizabeth.

'Sit here, Maddison,' said Mrs Scrimshaw,

pointing to a hard wooden chair, 'and no talking to Jepson.'

Rose and Elizabeth exchanged quick glances as Rose sat down. After a few minutes Elizabeth was called into the Board room. Rose strained her ears to hear. No sound came through the heavy wooden door, but there was the clatter of quick footsteps in the corridor.

'Maddison, stand up.' Mrs Scrimshaw was pulling at her arm. 'It's Dr Lowe.'

Barely acknowledging Mrs Scrimshaw, the doctor knocked briefly on the Boardroom door and bustled in, closing the door firmly behind him.

Almost immediately, the door opened again. Elizabeth came out with Mrs Clements, who beckoned to Rose. Mrs Scrimshaw tried to follow Rose into the room, but Mrs Clements shook her head.

'Stay here with Jepson,' she said.

Dr Lowe was already giving his evidence to the Board.

'Maddison gave the child laudanum to help her sleep, which is common practice,' Dr Lowe explained, 'especially with poor people. Laudanum's cheaper than gin or wine. It's very effective in quieting fretful babies or young children. Unfortunately it can have a harmful effect on the breathing, especially in children under two. In addition the child was already ailing. She had developed the chest infection, which affected a number of children on the jacketers' ward. The combination of respiratory problems and laudanum directly contributed to her death.'

He meant it was her fault then, thought Rose. *If she hadn't given Lucy the laudanum, she wouldn't have died.*

'In your opinion then, Dr Lowe, is this a matter of maternal neglect, or ... ' Mr Birch paused, ' ... a case of infanticide?'

Dr Lowe did not answer immediately. He bowed his head. All heads turned towards him, waiting for his reply. The only sound in the room was the ticking of the black marble clock on the mantelpiece.

Rose remembered the Master's words when she'd thrown the bread over the wall to Tom ... *anyone who commits an offence here may be sent before a Magistrate and sentenced to a term in prison if the offence is sufficiently serious*. Nothing could be more serious than a mother neglecting her child, or worse ...

Dr Lowe raised his head, cleared his throat and looked across at Rose.

'Although she's young, Maddison has always been a caring mother. In my considered opinion there's no question of neglect or infanticide.'

The men seated around the table remained silent.

'What do you all think, then?' Mr Birch gazed

round at their stern faces.

Rose felt herself sway. The room was so hot. She needed air. She felt an arm round her shoulders.

'Sit down.' Matron pulled a chair forward.

Rose sank down, gripping the arms of the chair, her hands sweaty but cold. Her breathing was quick and shallow. She heard the rumble of the men's voices, but couldn't bear to look at them. She kept her eyes closed and her head bent. It didn't matter what Dr Lowe said. She was a pauper and a troublemaker. She broke the rules. They would still send her to prison, not just the Punishment Cell, but a real prison. And then ... She felt frozen with fear.

Gradually the men's voices faded. The room was silent now, apart from the ticking of the clock. Rose opened her eyes, lifting her head just a fraction.

Mr Birch cleared his throat.

‘I think we are all in agreement, gentlemen?’

He looked around the table. Heads nodded.

‘Death by misadventure,’ he pronounced.

Misadventure ... what did that mean? She looked up at Matron.

‘An accident, Maddison, not your fault,’ Matron whispered.

Mr Birch turned to the Master. ‘What about the burial, Clements?’

‘The child will remain in the Mortuary until one of the able-bodied men, under the supervision of Scrimshaw, has prepared a grave in the Burial Ground. I will speak to Scrimshaw directly. I will order an elm coffin, of the appropriate size, from our usual contractor.’

He paused, and raised his voice, ‘Maddison, you should not have run away with your brother, but in the circumstances we will impose only a minor punishment. You will be confined in a separate room for twelve hours, and your diet will be bread and water. Thereafter you may return to your work.'

Tom's punishment was two days in the Punishment Cell, twelve hours each day, though he was allowed to return to the ward each night.

He and Rose longed to speak to their mother, but Scrimshaw kept a close watch on Tom, and Mrs Scrimshaw followed Rose everywhere. They would have to wait until Sunday afternoon to tell their mother why they had run away.

Eleven

On Friday morning Scrimshaw heard someone knocking on the door of his Lodge. A rough-looking man stood on the doorstep. His clothes were shabby, his boots dusty, his face lined.

'I want to see the Master,' he said.

'*I* deal with vagrants,' Scrimshaw said.

'I want to see the Master,' the man said more loudly. 'I'm no vagrant.'

'I'll be the judge of that.' Scrimshaw squared

his shoulders. 'The Master's busy. He's at the Board meeting.'

'Then I'll see him there.' The man shoved Scrimshaw back against the door and pushed past him.

'Come back!' Scrimshaw shouted, but he'd been winded, and the man was already half-way across the yard.

A woman carrying a bundle of sheets was coming towards them. The man ran up to her.

'Where's the Boardroom, missus?'

'Stop that vagrant!' Scrimshaw yelled.

'Through there.' The woman nodded towards the door at the far end of the yard. 'Then right, and right again.'

The man sped towards the door, pushed it open, turned right down the corridor, and then right again.

But Scrimshaw was getting closer. He was strong, and had recovered quickly from being winded. The stranger had walked many miles, all through the night, desperate to reach Fenbridge as soon as he could. He was breathing heavily as he ran towards the door at the end of the corridor.

Just as he reached the door and raised his right arm to knock, Scrimshaw came up from behind and grabbed the arm. Desperately the man tried to shake him off, but Scrimshaw's grip was tight. He grabbed the other arm and wrenched both arms behind the man's back. The man struggled to free himself, kicking out at Scrimshaw. The door opened, and the Master stood there. Behind him, the Guardians sat around the table, their heads turned towards the two men in the doorway.

'What is the meaning of this commotion?' the Master asked.

'He forced his way in,' Scrimshaw said. 'I told him he couldn't see you. He won't bother you no more. I'll throw him out. We've no room for the likes of him.'

He pushed the man and started to move away down the corridor. But the man had an unexpected ally. The Master had noticed on several occasions recently that Scrimshaw assumed more authority than he should.

'Wait,' he said. 'We'll hear the man. That'll be all, Scrimshaw. Return to your own duties.'

Scowling, Scrimshaw turned away, and the man followed the Master into the room.

'I left my wife and bairns,' Samuel told the Guardians, 'when we lost our tied cottage. I couldn't get work, see, and I thought they'd be better off without me. I thought the Union would do more for them if I weren't about.'

The Guardians regarded him sternly.

'I tried to get work, sirs. I'd have taken

anything, but it was no good. They won't pay a man's wage when a bairn can do the work, everybody knows that.'

Mr Grey, the farmer, nodded his head, 'That is the case.'

'I tramped from farm to farm,' Samuel said, 'and then from workhouse to workhouse. I was at Broughton, on my way back to Cranby, when I saw my bairns, Tom and Rose. I realised they'd been looking for me, so I thought to myself, maybe I can be with my family again, even if it's the workhouse for all of us.'

He paused and looked at the faces around the table. What were they thinking? Did they despise him, a man who'd left his wife and children?

'What was your trade, Maddison?' Mr Birch asked.

'I was a horseman, sir.'

'Were you a good one?' asked Squire Durrant.

'Aye, I were, sir. I worked eleven year for old

Henry Barnes, but then he died sudden. There were no sons to carry on the farm, and his widow didn't want it. She sold up the land and got rid of the horses, so I lost my work and my home. Nobody round here wanted another horseman.'

'You're right there,' Mr Grey said. 'I remember old Henry. Farm was sold Michaelmas before last. I bought two of his horses, and right good they've been. Well looked after, they were.'

He paused, looking Samuel up and down.

'I should think you look a deal better when you're cleaned up a bit.' He turned to the Chairman and the Master. 'Now, Birch, Clements, what d'you think of this? I could do with another horseman. Mine's getting on a bit now and can't manage so well as he did. I could take on Maddison here as second horseman, and there's plenty of work on the land for the boy. There's a cottage too. It's a bit run-down, been empty these last two years. The missus keeps her hens in there, but we can soon tidy it up for them.'

'That seems very satisfactory,' Mr Birch said. 'What d'you think, Clements?'

'I agree. Maddison and his family can support themselves then, with no need of any relief from the Union.'

'Quite so,' agreed Squire Durrant.

'An excellent solution,' murmured the Reverend Carter.

'And what do you think, Maddison?' Mr Grey asked.

'Yes, thank you, sir, yes,' said Samuel.

Twelve

It's Sunday morning. Rose and Tom come in through the open doorway. Rose carries a bundle of the kindling she's just been chopping, and drops it down on the hearth. Tom lugs a bucket of water that he's just pumped from the well.

The fire in the black range is lit, even though the sun is shining. A pan of broth bubbles on the hob. Their father whittles away at a reed. Their mother pauses as she stirs the soup. She turns to their father, wooden spoon in mid-air, smiling,

'Samuel Maddison, stop making that mess on my hearth!'

It's five months now since they left the workhouse. Life still isn't easy. They are poor and they all work hard, on the land and in the home. There are still days when Rose longs to hold Lucy in her arms. She misses her friends Harriet and Elizabeth, knowing she may never see them again. Lydia worries that she can't always put food on the table. Samuel and Tom fear the bleak winter months.

But the memories of the workhouse grow fainter. Now they have four rooms they can call their own, in the two-up and two-down cottage belonging to their employer, Mr Grey. They grow their own vegetables on the plot of land behind the cottage. Their pig snuffles in her sty at the end of the garden. Their chickens squawk and scratch in the dust.

They are together.

Author's Note

The Poor Law Amendment Act, 1834

When the Maddison family arrive at Fenbridge Workhouse one November night in 1838, the cruel Porter, Scrimshaw, tells them there is a 'new Poor Law' which 'stops idle folk coming in here to live off the Parish in the lap of luxury while decent, hard-working souls struggle to earn a crust.'

Scrimshaw is referring to the Poor Law Amendment Act of 1834*. Until then, poor people in Great Britain were provided for under the Old Poor Law, based on an act passed over 260 years earlier, in the reign of Queen Elizabeth I.

Before 1834 it was the duty of every parish to provide financial support for their own poor, sick and elderly. The money was raised through a compulsory poor rate, a type of property tax. The parishioners who paid it complained that the money went to those who were poor because of their own failings; they were too lazy to work, and had too many children.

Another frequent criticism, but from a different point of view, was that employers deliberately kept their workers' wages low because they knew their workers would be supplemented by Parish Relief, under the old Poor Law.

---

* The legislation I have described here relates to England and Wales; separate, but similar, Acts were passed in Scotland.

Supporters of the new 1834 Poor Law believed the poor were undeserving and that poverty was the individual's fault. They ignored the social and economic conditions of the early nineteenth century that contributed to poverty – the increase in the population of the working class; the return of huge numbers of soldiers from the Napoleonic wars; the beginning of the industrial revolution; more efficient farming methods resulting in fewer jobs and lower wages; and the Corn Laws, imposing high import duties on cereals from other countries in order to protect English farmers from foreign competition and keep the price of bread high.

The Poor Law Amendment Act was intended to cut costs. Poor people would no longer be given financial help to remain in their own homes. If they wanted help they had to go into the workhouse and work there for their food and clothing. The conditions in the workhouse were intended to be a deterrent, so harsh that no one would want to go there, certainly not the idle poor. Only those who were absolutely destitute, like Lydia Maddison and her children, would apply for admission to the workhouse.

The Poor Law Commission for England and Wales was set up with three commissioners, whose job was to form unions of groups of parishes to provide poor relief. Boards of Guardians, like the one for Fenbridge Workhouse, were elected by the ratepayers and property owners to administer these unions and provide workhouse accommodation for paupers in their area.

Sometimes existing workhouses were adapted; more often, new workhouses had to be built. They needed to be large enough to accommodate several hundred men, women and children. Usually they were built in isolated locations, as nobody wanted a workhouse on their doorstep.

The Boards of Guardians met together, weekly or fortnightly, to make decisions about financial matters, the maintenance of the workhouse building, improvements to the building, diet, discipline, and the appointment of workhouse officers. Local representatives of the Poor Law Commission, assistant Poor Law Commissioners, regularly visited the workhouses to inspect them.

On their arrival at Fenbridge Workhouse, Lydia, Rose and Tom are especially upset when Scrimshaw tells them that they are going to be separated from each other in the workhouse, and will not be allowed to live together as a family. Under the old Poor Law, married couples and families had been able to live together in the workhouse. After the 1834 Act they were to be split up, segregated, into separate dormitories – men in one, women and children under seven in another, and children over seven in another. Unmarried mothers and their babies were to be segregated from everyone else, as were vagrants (tramps).

Charles Dickens and 'Oliver Twist'

At the time, many people supported the new Poor Law, but there were others who strongly opposed it, such as the writer, Charles Dickens. Dickens had real experience of poverty: his father had been imprisoned for debt when Dickens was a child. At the time of the Poor Law Amendment Act Dickens was a newspaper reporter, and in the summer of 1834 he attended many debates in Parliament on proposed amendments to the Poor Law. Although several MPs objected to the amendments, the new bill was passed.

These parliamentary debates were probably the inspiration for Dickens' novel *Oliver Twist*, sub-titled *The Parish Boy's Progress*. This was published as a serial in monthly instalments (rather like our modern TV soaps) in a magazine called *Bentley's Miscellany*, between February 1837 and April 1839. It was also published in book form at the end of 1838, around the time the Maddisons were admitted to Fenbridge workhouse.

It is extremely unlikely that a family such as the Maddison family would have read *Bentley's Miscellany*, with Dickens' vivid account of Oliver Twist's experiences in the workhouse. But some members of the Board of Guardians at Fenbridge may well have done, for instance the kindly farmer, Mr Grey, and Squire Durrant and Reverend Carter. Doctor Lowe, who tells the Board that Rose was 'a caring mother', may also have been a subscriber to *Bentley's*. This was the audience that Charles Dickens was trying to speak to in his stories.

The stigma of the workhouse

Poor people became very afraid of 'ending up in the workhouse', and felt stigmatised by the word *pauper*. Although the word could mean simply 'a poor person' it tended to have the additional meaning of being destitute, without means of livelihood – a beggar, depending on charity or public welfare, such as poor law relief. People labelled 'paupers' felt a sense of shame and disgrace. The impression given by Scrimshaw is that because the Maddisons were paupers, they had no rights at all.

Fear of the workhouse, and all it represented, lasted right through Queen Victoria's reign (1837 to 1901) and into the twentieth century. The Poor Law system was reformed, attitudes towards the causes of poverty were changing and a different approach to social welfare was developing, but still people, especially older people, feared 'ending up in the workhouse'.

Was the workhouse totally bad?

As a social reformer, Dickens wanted to draw his readers' attention to the ills of society as he saw them, for example, cruelty to poor children, the evils of child labour and the criminalisation of street children. He was keen to persuade his readers of the failings of the new Poor Law. So in his stories he drew a somewhat over-simplified picture, emphasising the cruelty and harshness of the workhouse.

The regime in the workhouses was certainly strict, discipline was severe, punishments were harsh, the working day was long, the work (mostly manual) was hard, and the diet was frugal, limited and monotonous. In some workhouses there was certainly cruelty and abuse.

As in all institutions (such as the schools, hospitals, care homes, and prisons of today) there were differences between individual workhouses, between individual members of workhouse staff, and between individual guardians. Some inmates (such as children, the old and the sick) were treated with more compassion.

In this story we can see that at Fenbridge there are differences in the way individual members of staff behave towards the people in their care. The Scrimshaws, for example, show no kindness or sympathy towards any of the Maddison family. In fact, Mrs Scrimshaw, Assistant Matron, is especially harsh towards Rose because she is an unmarried mother.

However, although the Master, Mr Clements, and the Matron, Mrs Clements, are strict, they do try to be fair. You may also have noticed some small instances of individual acts of kindness from other members of the workhouse staff.

The workhouse meals were certainly monotonous, but they were regular and reasonably nutritious. Lydia, Rose and Tom all benefit from a better diet than the one they had before they came to Fenbridge. The workhouse school often provided a better education than children outside the workhouse received, as there was no system of compulsory State Education at that time.

For most families though, as for the Maddisons, any positive aspects of the workhouse were overshadowed by the fact that they could not live together as a family. What Mr Grey, the farmer, offers Samuel, Lydia, Tom and Rose is what most people wanted (and still want) – regular work, financial independence, their own home – the freedom to be together.

Some of the negative attitudes to poor people behind the Poor Law Amendment Act are still with us today – the idea that poor people are always cheats, lazy, 'getting away with it' and 'need to be taught a lesson'.

How do you think our society should help people who lack the resources to look after themselves?

Never Odd or Even

by John Townsend

'I'm at that special age: 12. It's one of my favourite numbers. 12 isn't just the sum of 10 (the base of our whole amazing number system) and 2 (the only even prime number in the universe) but it's the first number with 1, 2, 3 and 4 as factors. I reckon that's so cool.'

Here's a detective story with a difference. Eliot is twelve – and he thinks outside the box. He can't help it. Numbers are his thing – and letters. So when 'the biggest mystery that struck our school in the history of the world' needs to be solved, Eliot is the one to call on.

But this time the solution doesn't lie in the real world (or in the 'real' world of the story). Instead, the solution lies *inside the book* itself – only it's locked away in a series of puzzles and palindromes.

Can you spot the hidden clues and find the culprit?

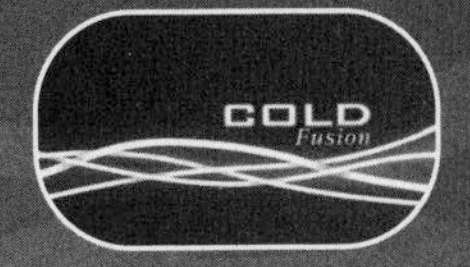

The Secret Message

by John Townsend

In the attic of his house, Sam finds a leather case that belonged to his great great grandfather, Freddy Ovel. The case contains a diary, and as Sam begins to read it, he is taken right back to just before the First World War, when Freddy was a boy. Sam also finds a photograph and discovers that at his age, Freddy was his exact double.

The diary unlocks more than just the events of the war, however. Sam discovers there is much more to 'Freddy' than meets the eye – not only heroic wartime deeds and terrible injuries, but also some very dark secrets indeed.

This poignant story, spanning a century, is the perfect way to remember the outbreak of the first great war of our times.